The People
of the Cave

PEOPLE OF THE CAVE
Adapted by: Murteza al-Albani & Zuka R. Qalaji
Illustrations: Terry Norridge 2001

A CIP record for this title is available from the British Library

ISBN 0-86037-301-0

Published by
The Islamic Foundation, Markfield Conference Centre
Ratby Lane, Markfield, Leicestershire LE67 9SY, United Kingdom
Tel: (01530) 244944 Fax: (01530) 244946
E-mail: i.foundation@islamic-foundation.org.uk

Quran House, PO Box 30611, Nairobi, Kenya

PMB 3193, Kano, Nigeria

Acknowledgments
The Islamic Foundation thanks the following in the publication of this book:
Sister Fatima D'Oyen
Sister Michele Messaoudi
Brother Nait Attia for his original cover concept

The People
of the Cave

Adapted by
Murteza al-Albani
and
Zuka R. Qalaji

*In the name of Allah, the Most Compassionate,
the Most Merciful*

Dear Parents,

As-salamu 'alaykum wa rahmatullahi wa barakatuhu.

The People of the Cave was originally written in Arabic as one in a series of books for Muslim youth. This is an English adaptation of one of these highly popular stories of Islam.

Many children in the Arabic-speaking world know these tales by heart, since they are a delight to the imagination and instructive to the mind and soul. As a result, the idea came to publish these books so that a wider English-speaking young Muslim audience could benefit from them, just as Arab children have for this past decade or longer.

The People of the Cave is not just an imaginative story. Care has been taken to include accurate information about Islamic concepts and historical facts. We pray that it will be of benefit to you, and be a source of inspiration to you for years to come, *insha' Allah.*

May Allah guide and protect us all. *Amin.*

Murteza al-Albani and Zuka R. Qalaji

In the name of Allah, the Most Compassionate,
the Most Merciful

Dear Reader,

As-salamu 'alaykum wa rahmatullahi wa barakatuhu.

This book is translated from the original Arabic, and adapted for young English-speaking Muslims.

Murteza al-Albani was born and brought up in the USA, as were his parents. He has taught English in schools and universities. Murteza knows the problems affecting Muslims living in non-Muslim countries, as he has lived through them himself. Zuka R. Qalaji studied Arabic, Islamic Sciences and History in Syria.

Growing up as a Muslim requires knowledge of the *din*, so you can do your best with your life. In this book we hope, *insha' Allah*, you will find good material that you can use in your daily life, so as to get the best reward from Allah.

The People of the Cave is fun to read, as thousands of Arab youth have found. We are sure that you will both enjoy and learn from this story, and we pray that Allah guides and blesses you. *Amin.*

Chapter 1

THUD! The three brothers tumbled to the floor and giggled uncontrollably. They had just walked home after performing the afternoon prayer in the mosque, and were now playing in their bedroom instead of having their afternoon nap, as is the custom in the Arab world. Their mother, awakened unexpectedly from her much-needed rest, became upset when she heard the boys' laughter echoing throughout the house.

"Go to sleep, boys!" she called out from her bedroom, wearily. "Sleep like the People of the Cave!" But instead of calming down, Muhammad, the eight year old, continued to wrestle with his twelve-year-old brother, Ali.

Abdullah, who was fourteen and the eldest, scolded his younger brothers: "You two had better be quiet! You know better than to bother Mama while she's sleeping! Baba is coming home soon, and you're going to be in trouble!"

"Yeah, well you were making a noise too!" answered Muhammad.

Just then, the boys heard the sound of footsteps and jingling keys.

"It's Baba!" shouted Muhammad and Ali together, forgetting their conversation with Abdullah as they raced to open the door. In their glee, they nearly toppled their father as he entered. Ali grabbed his father's right hand while Muhammad tugged on his left. Hearing the commotion, their mother had joined them, having given up the idea of getting

any more rest that day.

"*As-salamu 'alaykum,*" said their mother, greeting their father with a smile as he entered the sitting room. The boys joined in giving their greetings.

"*Wa-'alaykum as-salam,*" replied their father warmly, pausing briefly to greet his wife before taking his usual place in his favourite armchair, with the boys gathered around him.

The sight of the boys sitting happily with their father quickly melted any remaining irritation in their mother's heart. She shook her head with a smile. "I'm going to the kitchen now, to get dinner started. If you need anything, let me know."

"Thank you, dear," replied their father as their mother disappeared into the other room.

Suddenly Ali remembered something his mother had said earlier. "Baba," he asked curiously, "Mama wants us to sleep like the People of the Cave, but who are they and how did they sleep?" His brothers shared his puzzled expression. Their father wondered at their question. He also wondered why they were asking him, since their mother was the one who had mentioned them.

Suddenly, with a flash of understanding, he asked with a teasing grin: "Why didn't you ask your mother?"

"I was going to, but I didn't get a chance," said Ali, hesitating and looking down at the floor, sheepishly.

"And might that have been because you woke her up from her nap?"

Father looked straight at him.

"I suppose so," admitted Ali.

"We were just playing," Muhammad chimed in, "and we didn't mean to wake up Mama from her nap. We had already done our homework and said our prayers."

"I told them to be quiet, but they kept on making a noise, even after Mama told them to stop," explained Abdullah in frustration.

"But don't we have the right to play after a long day's work?" Muhammad asked, boldly.

Their father responded patiently. "Yes, you may play," he said. "But you must also know your limits. You know how much effort your mother makes on your behalf. Remember, the Prophet Muhammad ﷺ taught us that if the mother is pleased with her children, they will enter Paradise. And if not, …well, they might not. I believe an apology is in order."

The boys became quiet and looked down at the floor. Ali

was drawing imaginary circles on the carpet; Muhammad put his hand to his chin and reflected on what his father had said. Then Abdullah looked up.

"I'm sorry, Baba," he said in a low voice. "I'm the eldest and I should have set a good example. I shouldn't have let them make a noise in the first place."

"I'm pleased that you're admitting your mistake, Abdullah. Allah loves those who are humble and repent for whatever wrong they have done. Now, what do you think you should do about it?"

"Well, I can begin by asking Mama to forgive me," answered Abdullah, with sudden resolve.

"And I'm going to help her with the housework, too," volunteered Ali.

"You can all help her with preparing dinner, and with the cleaning up," responded their father.

On the verge of tears, Muhammad said with all his heart: "We love Mama dearly. Do you think she will forgive us?"

Their father smiled and lifted up his youngest son, giving him a big hug. "Your mother is a kind-hearted woman. I'm sure that she'll forgive you. However, you've got to ask her first. And don't forget the story of the man who asked the Prophet ﷺ who, of all people, should receive his utmost respect and care."

"Yes, we've heard it many times," admitted Abdullah.

Young Muhammad asked, "Is that the one where the man asked the Prophet ﷺ the same question three times, and each time he answered: 'Your mother'?"

"Yes," replied their father. "And the blessed Prophet didn't answer 'Your father' until the man had asked the same question for the fourth time."

Muhammad grinned and turned to his brothers who, judging from their similar grins, seemed to be thinking the same thing he was. Ali turned to his father.

"You just decided for us, Baba, that we should listen more to Mama than to you!"

Their good-natured father laughed along with his sons at their joke. Then, becoming serious once again, he said, "Alright, run along now. You know what you have to do."

Chapter 2

"Mama, we are very sorry. Please forgive us," pleaded Muhammad as he entered the kitchen. "We promise we won't do it again," added Abdullah.

"Yes, please don't be angry with us. We won't be able to go to Paradise!" Ali blurted out.

"What?" asked their mother, surprised at Ali's comment. "Who told you that?"

"Baba did. He was reminding us of what the Prophet ﷺ said, about treating mothers with respect."

Their mother blushed and smiled. Drying her hands, she gave each of them a kiss on his forehead, followed by a little hug. She had to get up on her toes to reach Abdullah, who had shot up in height during the past year and was now taller than she was. "Of course I forgive you," she said, warmly. "Just try to remember to be quiet when I'm taking my nap. Sometimes I stay up until late at night, and I need to catch up on my sleep during the day."

Abdullah turned to his brothers, suddenly remembering something. "Hey, did you know that Mama often gets up in the middle of the night to pray *salat al-tahajjud*, and then she stays up to read the Qur'an?"

"Do you, Mama?" asked Ali.

"What's *salat al-tahajjud*?" added Muhammad, curiously.

"*Salat al-tahajjud* is the prayer that the Prophet ﷺ recommended people to pray late at night," answered Abdullah. "Isn't it, Mum?" he added.

"Yes, Abdullah; that's right."

"But isn't it hard to get up in the middle of the night?" asked Ali, who had trouble waking up for the dawn prayer.

"Well, the time of night before dawn is a blessed time. It's special; the Qur'an says so. I always feel at peace throughout the day when I manage to get up to pray *tahajjud.*" Turning to stir the delicious-smelling food that was starting to bubble in the pot, she added, "You boys don't worry about my nap any longer. I've got to get to work, so that we can eat on time."

"But we've come to help you," explained Abdullah, as he started to wash some dishes that had been left over from lunch.

"Yeah, and we're going to set the table, aren't we, Muhammad?" added Ali as he looked for the plates.

"Yes, and then will you please tell us the story of the People of the Cave?" asked Muhammad, who was always eager for a good story.

"Well," said their mother, "your father is a better storyteller than I am. Why don't we ask him to tell it to us after dinner?"

After enjoying a delicious meal and performing their *maghrib* prayers, the family settled down comfortably in the sitting room. "I understand that you boys would like to hear the story of the People of the Cave. Is that right?" asked their father with a twinkle in his eye.

"Yes! Please tell us the story," pleaded Muhammad. "Why were they sleeping in a cave? What were they doing there?" The boys looked to their father with eyes wide open, filled with anticipation.

Chapter 3

"The People of the Cave lived thousands of years ago," their father began. "Some say they lived in the northernmost part of Syria called Tarsus which has high, rugged mountains. It is halfway between the cities of Aleppo and Antakya, which is in Turkey. Others say that they lived in Ephesus, which is south of the Turkish city of Izmir. What matters most is that they all were good *mu'minin*, because they believed in the One God, Allah, and not in other gods and idols, as many people of their city did at the time. In their intentions and deeds, these young men always followed the straight path."

"Excuse me, Baba, but how do we know about their story?" Ali asked, always eager to learn.

"Allah tells us the main points of their story in *Surah Al-Kahf*, which is Chapter 18 in the Qur'an," answered his father. "The Qur'an emphasizes the moral of the story, although some people have tried to investigate the historical details regarding it. In fact, there were many legends in the Prophet's ﷺ day about the 'Seven Sleepers', as they were known. *Surah Al-Kahf* was revealed in response to three questions put to the Prophet ﷺ by some Jews of Madinah. They wanted to know what the Prophet ﷺ would say about some controversial stories and legends of the past, and one of their questions was about the People of the Cave."

Their father's face began to display the special dreamy expression he got when he started to tell them a story.

Although their father was a good Muslim and didn't say anything that would contradict something in the Qur'an or Sunnah, he didn't see any harm in adding a few imaginative details to make the story more interesting. He felt his sons would remember the stories better that way.

"Imagine, my sons, an evil king who didn't believe in Allah and who hated people like the young *mu'minin* (believers) of this city. This evil ruler was most likely one of the ancient Roman kings, many of whom were tyrants. Wherever he went, he tried to force people to leave the right path. He wanted them to stop worshipping the One True God and to follow the Romans, who believed in many gods and idols. The king's heart was full of hatred for believers, because they refused to follow his way. He tried to bribe the believers by offering them money and powerful positions, in exchange for obeying him. But faithful believers everywhere refused. The king responded by putting them in prison and torturing them. Afterwards he executed them."

"He didn't have the right to do that!" shouted Abdullah in anger at the injustice.

"Well, my son, it is a fact that disbelievers in powerful positions, like the king, often feel that they can simply order others to do what they believe is correct. They think that nobody has the right to refuse their orders, or even to discuss them. In truth, they are ignorant people. If they had any real knowledge, they would realise that they're not gaining anything except the anger of Allah."

"Baba, could you continue the story, please?" asked Muhammad impatiently. "I can't wait to hear what happened next!"

Their father resumed. "As I said, the king used to travel to many places to try to force people into changing their faith. One day, the evil king passed through the city where the young believers of our story lived. He ordered his soldiers to search the city and gather all believers in the One God before him."

"Bring them to me!" said their father in his scariest and most imposing voice, "I shall imprison those I wish and shall execute those I wish! No one can stop me! "

The boys smiled at their father's impersonation of the evil king. Their father continued.

"The king's soldiers captured the young men. There were only a few of them – between three and seven, perhaps – young men not much older than you boys, in their mid-to-late teens. People throughout history used to speculate and argue about how many believers there were, but the Qur'an teaches that their number is not important. Quality is more important than quantity. Now at first, the king asked the young people to give up their belief in Allah. Then he offered them wealth and power, as a bribe. Finally, he threatened them:

"If you refuse, you will get nothing but the edge of my sword upon your neck!"

By this time, Muhammad was growing anxious. He put his trembling fingers to his mouth to calm himself down. Ali drew closer to him to comfort him, even though he, too, feared for their lives. Their father noticed their reaction to his story, and smiled.

"My dear sons, these young believers were not afraid, because their faith was strong. One of them confidently replied to the evil king:

'Our faith is more valuable to us than life itself. Your threat means nothing to us, because life and death belong only to Allah, who created everything and everyone, including you and me. Since all people must die one day, it is better for us to die as believers and gain eternal life in Paradise, than to change to your idolatry and burn in Hell.' "

Muhammad smiled and looked relieved.

"What happened after that? Did he kill them?" Ali asked his father.

"No. When they refused his offer, the evil king said that they were too young to be executed. He told them that he would not kill them. However, he threatened them once again. He said he was going away to another country and would return after a few months. If they did not abandon their faith by then, he would decide what to do about them."

"Maybe he thought that because they were young, they could easily be pressured into giving up their faith," mused Abdullah.

"They wouldn't, would they Baba?" asked Muhammad, somewhat doubtful.

"No, Muhammad," their father chuckled. "Their faith was too strong for that, *al-hamdulillah.*"

"Then what did they do?" asked Ali.

Now their father's mastery of the storytelling skills they all loved became apparent as he continued, using a variety of voices and gestures. His eyes gleamed as he said, "Well, they held *shura* (consultation) – they all got together to discuss the situation.

The first one said: 'We must make our escape before the king returns!'

The second one answered: 'But where can we go?'

A third replied: 'We can live in the mountains and keep our faith. It is better than living here, as disbelievers.'

A fourth young man responded: 'Yes, I agree. Living a simple life close to nature while keeping true to our faith is many times better than a life of comfort without it. My mother suggested that we go to a cave far up in the mountains, where we could live without being discovered. I know of one that I found years ago, when I used to herd goats.'

The second one said: 'That sounds good. How are we going to survive up there? We'll need food and water.'

The fourth believer replied: 'We can carry some supplies with us, and tools for fishing and hunting. The area is full of wildlife, and there is a small stream not too far from the cave, where we can get water. We should also take as many silver coins as we can, just in case.'

The first one said: 'So that settles it! Let's not waste any time. Let each of us gather whatever supplies and money he can. We can meet behind the big boulder at the outskirts of the city, before dawn. Our brother the goatherd will be our guide.'

'It will be my pleasure,' the fourth believer replied. 'May Allah guide us and make us successful, and grant victory to all the believers.'

'*Amin!*' they responded in unison. 'Allah be with you, brother' they said to one another, as they shook hands and embraced before departing on their mission."

Chapter 4

"At the crack of dawn, when the eastern horizon was just faintly pink, the young believers quietly left their homes to gather at the big rock. From there they began to make their way along little-known mountain paths to the cave, hoping to arrive there before sunrise. Although they tried to avoid being seen by anyone, they unexpectedly came across an old shepherd and his dog in the woods. At first they were alarmed, but he soon put them at ease.

'Hey, there!' said the old man as he examined their faces, one by one. 'You boys wouldn't be up to any mischief, would you? By the looks of you, I would judge you to be honest

young men, but what are you doing in these parts at this hour, and with all that gear?'

"The oldest believer spoke up. 'No, we mean no harm. We have fled the city and are seeking refuge in the hills. We are fleeing from the evil king.'

"And so they confided in him, and told him of their plight. They also spoke to him about the One God, Allah, and invited him to put his faith in Allah alone, rather than in idols. The shepherd pondered seriously over their words, while his dog sat patiently beside him. The young believers waited, almost holding their breath, and silently prayed while the shepherd remained deep in thought for some time. Suddenly the old man stood up and declared his faith in Allah.

'From now on I will have nothing to do with idolatry. I have often thought that nature was too vast and beautiful, and life too full of wonder to be under the control of gods of wood and stone, fashioned by the hands of men. Thank you for making clear to me what I knew in my soul all along,' the old man said, with tears in his eyes.

The young men rejoiced and prayed for their new brother in faith."

"Baba, the boys were trying to escape death," said Abdullah. "How did they think of taking the time to invite the shepherd to worship Allah? And how did they have the courage to be so open about their mission?"

Their father answered earnestly, "As believers, they cherished their faith so much that their main concern was to please Allah. Believers find happiness in spreading Allah's word. They are elated when they find someone who listens and accepts the Truth."

"What happened next, Baba?" asked Muhammad.

"Well, the shepherd decided to give his dog to the young men.

'You boys will need his protection more than I do. Take him with you and he will guard you well,' he generously offered.

'But we couldn't do that,' protested one of them. 'What would you do without your dog?'

'I have two more dogs back home. Take him, in Allah's name, and may he serve you well.'

"After praising Allah and taking their leave of the old shepherd, the young believers made their way to the cave. They quickly set up house, arranging their food, supplies and bedding. They collected firewood, made traps, wove mats and baskets, and soon had a cosy, simple home. Before and after their daily tasks, they filled their hours with prayer and studying the scriptures. And they took joy in the awesome majesty of the natural world around them: the breathtaking sunrises and sunsets, the songs of the birds and antics of the squirrels, the fresh mountain air scented with the perfume of wild flowers, the babbling brook. They would have remained there happily for many years if they had not run into trouble," their father concluded.

Muhammad asked, "Why, what happened, Baba?"

Chapter 5

"There came a time when they were almost out of food, and they had not caught any wild game for some time. They decided that one of them should go down to the city to buy more food and supplies, and bring back any news of the evil king. One was chosen, and he agreed to go to an area of the city where he was least likely to be recognised. After receiving further instructions, advice and their prayers for success, he made his way back to the city, alone.

'Good day,' greeted the youth, as he walked into a shop. 'I'll be needing a large sack of grain, and some oil, and salt…' he continued, naming some other necessities.

'Getting ready for a long journey, eh?' asked the shopkeeper, curiously. The boy blushed.

'Well, um, yes – I mean, no, not exactly… I am…' he stammered, as he tried to change the subject. 'I've been out of town for some time, and am eager for any news. What's happening in the city? Is there any news of the king?'

'The king has been back for a month now,' replied the shopkeeper, eyeing him closely. 'Your face looks familiar, boy. Don't I know you from somewhere? I think I've seen you at the palace.

You wouldn't be a deserter from the army, now, would you?' he asked, his eyes narrowing.

'Me, a deserter?' the young believer replied, 'Oh, no, I've never been in the army. I was just curious,' he said, nervously."

Ali and Muhammad shifted uncomfortably in their seats as their father continued his story.

"When he had purchased the food and supplies he left quickly, dodging from one street to another, hoping that he wasn't being followed. The shopkeeper's questions had made him nervous, and he didn't trust him. He hurried back to the cave to warn the others. When he returned, the young believers expressed concern that the shopkeeper might have informed the king, or set someone on his trail. It might only be a matter of time before their hiding place was discovered. They pondered over their predicament, and consulted one another about what to do.

The first one said: 'In this matter, nobody can help us except Allah.'

The second replied: 'Yes, you are right, brother. Allah will not abandon us.'

The third one said: 'Let us pray to Allah to help us. Allah Who has power over all things, will give us strength to deal with whatever comes our way.' "

At this point, their father paused. He looked very closely at each of his three sons.

"These young people," he said, stressing every word, "understood the way of a believer. In everything that happened to them good or bad, they turned to Allah. The beloved Prophet ﷺ once said, '*Wondrous is the case of the believer, for there is good for him in everything, and so it is for him alone. If he encounters good, he is grateful to Allah, and that is good for him; and if he encounters difficulties he is patient, and that is good for him.*' Remember that," their father said, earnestly.

"What happened next, Baba?" asked Muhammad again, in a pleading voice.

"Well, Muhammad, they prayed to Allah," said their father, smiling at his young son's eagerness. "They said, 'O our Lord, grant us mercy from Your presence, and guide us to right conduct in our plight.'

"Then, Allah's peace descended on them and the worry left their hearts, and all of them – the dog included – fell asleep. The dog lay down at the entrance, his two front paws stretched towards the light entering the cave. It was very hot, and the air in the cave was stifling. Then a miracle occurred. Allah prevented the sun's rays from entering the cave, so that everyone inside stayed cool."

"How do we know that?" asked Ali.

Their father replied, "The Qur'an says:

And you might have seen the sun when it rose, move away from their cave to their right, and when it set go past them on the left, and they were in the open space between.

That was (one) of the signs of Allah.

"But this was no ordinary sleep," their father continued. "The young believers were preserved there just as they were, for a very long time, because Allah had a special plan for them."

"How long did they sleep?" asked Ali, curiously.

"Well, it is said that they slept for three hundred years, and Allah knows best. Some people said it was three hundred years; that is according to the solar or Gregorian calendar that many people use today. Others said 'three hundred and

nine years', which would be the same period of time reckoned by the lunar calendar, the calendar that we Muslims also use."

"Wow!" said Muhammad, "can you imagine that, being asleep for three hundred years!"

"It wouldn't be fun – you'd miss all the big matches," joked Ali, who was an enthusiastic football fan.

"*Subhanallah!*" said Abdullah seriously, ignoring Ali's remark. Then, remembering the earlier events of the day, he thought of a joke of his own: "I hope you don't really want us to sleep like the People of the Cave, Mama!"

His mother laughed, and responded warmly, "Not really, Abdullah. You boys snore too much, anyway. It would be very noisy around here!"

"Yeah," said Ali, "poor Mama – we're even noisy in our sleep!" They all laughed together.

Then Muhammad protested, "You interrupt too much! I want to hear the end of the story! Please continue, Baba!" he said.

"Alright, Muhammad. We've almost reached the end; be patient. When the young believers finally awoke, they felt strangely different, but they couldn't understand why. They were still in the cave, their dog was still there, but things seemed different, somehow.

'How long do you think we've been sleeping here?,' the first one said, still yawning.

'Maybe for a day, or half a day,' answered the second, rubbing his eyes.

The third one said: 'Allah knows best how long we've been sleeping, but I am very hungry. Is there anything to eat?'

"The fourth one went to check on their supplies, but found

that their grain seemed to have gone stale, and almost everything else was missing. The dried berries they had collected had all vanished. Even their salt pot had been overturned, and was empty. The tracks of small animals dotted the cave. Then they looked outside. The landscape looked different. Some trees outside the cave seemed much larger, a few of the biggest ones had fallen down, and many small trees were there that they had not noticed before. They looked down at the valley far below, and it seemed that the road to the city was wider than it had been, and the houses didn't look quite right. They couldn't understand it. They looked at each other in wonder.

'There's nothing we can do but go back to town to buy some more supplies,' said one, shaking his head, genuinely puzzled.

"Oh, what will they do if the king finds them…" Muhammad said, fearfully.

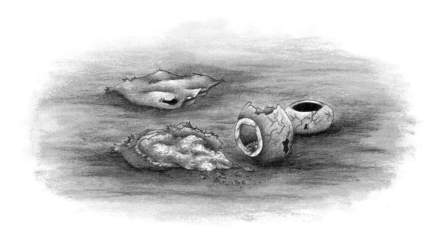

"Well, if they slept for three hundred years, the king would have been long dead by then, wouldn't he, Baba?" said Abdullah.

"Yes, son, that's right. That was Allah's way of saving them from the king's persecution. But that's not all," he continued.

The boys were listening attentively. Their father paused for a moment, then said:

"You must always remember the advice of our beloved Prophet ﷺ, 'If all the people gathered together to harm you, no one could harm you unless it was Allah's will. And if all the people gathered to help you, no one could help you unless it was Allah's will.'"

The boys nodded their heads, eager for their father to continue the story.

Chapter 6

"Now, the same young man decided to go back to the city, this time to a different shop. He noticed that many streets seemed to have changed, and the people dressed differently. He tried to blend in with the crowd, to avoid attracting attention to himself. He quietly chose the food and supplies he wanted, making sure that they were *halal,* and then handed over the silver coins he had with him. When the shopkeeper saw them, he was very surprised, because the coins were ancient relics that were no longer in use. Then, the shopkeeper looked more closely at the young man and noticed that his clothes looked strangely old-fashioned. 'Like

the shirts that my great-grandfather used to wear,' he mused to himself.

'Where did you get this money from, boy?' the shopkeeper asked, continuing to examine his strange customer.

'It is mine,' replied the young man quickly, although he sensed that something was wrong.

"The shopkeeper began to think that his customer might be a thief, or a grave-robber – one of those people of ill-repute who enrich themselves by digging up and selling the things that people sometimes bury with their dead."

"That's disgusting!" said Ali.

"Be quiet!" said Muhammad, giving his brother a little push with his shoulder.

Their father gave both of them a look which meant "settle down, boys", and they did. Then he continued.

"Our brave young man, anxious not to be detained any longer, politely said, 'Well, I really must be going. Thank you very much for your help, and you can keep the change.'

"Not so fast," said the shopkeeper, holding him by the shoulder. "Where do you come from, boy? Your accent sounds strange."

"Why, I come from this city," he replied. "I've lived here almost all my life. I'm no stranger here."

"A likely story!" the shopkeeper replied. "I'm taking you to our ruler!" he decided, firmly. "He is a wise man and always seeks the truth of matters."

"The young believer was perplexed. He thought that this man must be a loyal servant of the evil king, yet he didn't seem like a bad person. He struggled to get away from his captor, but soon found himself surrounded by a group of men, led by the shopkeeper, who were intent on taking him to the palace. There was nothing else to do but to go with them."

"May Allah help you if you are a thief!" the shopkeeper said as he led the young man into the king's chamber. The shopkeeper told the king what he knew of the young man's story.

The king listened patiently, and then addressed the young man before him:

"Thanks to our brother, the shopkeeper, who is a good believer and responsible citizen, you have been brought here to answer for yourself. Come closer, young man. Who are you, where are you from, and where did you get these coins?"

"At first, the young believer didn't dare look into the ruler's face. Then he wondered, because the voice sounded much kinder than the voice of the king he had known before.

He said: 'I am from this city, from the family of carpet-weavers. The coins are my own.'

The king replied: 'But there have been no weavers in this city for many years; since the last of them died of the plague, we have begun to import our carpets from the east.'

'But that's impossible,' said the young man, confused. 'This doesn't make any sense. I know many people here. Birunis, the owner of the vineyards; Kastonis, the teacher; and Kabus, the miller.'

The king said: 'Those are pagan Roman names, no longer favoured by our people. And our miller's name is Yaqub. Don't make up stories boy, it won't help you,' the king warned. 'Now tell the truth: where did you get these coins? Did you steal them?'

The believer said: 'No, I swear I did not steal them. They

are mine. My father gave them to me only a few months ago.'

'A few months ago?' the king replied, unbelievingly.

'It is the truth,' replied the believer, now distraught. With tears in his eyes, he said: 'It is the only truth I know.'

The king looked at him more kindly now, and with awe: 'Young man, your money is ancient. No one has used these coins for hundreds of years!'

"By this time", their father explained, "of course the young believer realised that he was somehow in the presence of a different ruler, in a changed city. He could not contain his anxiety. He asked, 'Please, your majesty, help me to understand this mystery. Who are you?'

The king said: 'Why, I am the king of this city, and this whole region. Everyone knows that.'

The young man said: 'The king? But what happened to the evil king, who was persecuting all those who rejected idolatry?'

The king said: 'He died a long, long time ago. He and his followers will fuel the fire of hell, because of their evil deeds. These days, *al-hamdulillah*, everyone in our city is a believer and worships Allah alone.'

The young man shook his head. 'The evil king, dead for a long time…? All the people worship Allah…?'

'Come here, young man. Come sit beside me and tell me your whole story, from beginning to end.'

"So the young man told the king his story, simply and with such conviction that no one could doubt he was telling the truth.

The king said: 'Can it be that you are one of the young men of long ago, who fled from the evil king? One of the people we heard legends about when we were children at our mother's knee, who have now woken up from a long sleep? This is strange indeed!'

The young man replied: 'I do not know. Allah knows best.'

'Where are the others who fled to the cave along with you?' the king asked.

'They are waiting there for me to return with food and supplies, sire.'

'Let us go to the cave so that I can meet them and welcome them. People who have such faith should be visited by kings,' he said.

'As you wish,' said the young man, humbly. 'I am at your service.'

Chapter 7

"Imagine, boys," said their father, "the king and the young believer walked together, accompanied by the king's soldiers, up the mountain to the cave. When they came to the cave's opening, the king told the young man to enter first."

'You go in, and tell the others to come out so that we can speak together in the sunlight.'

'Yes, sire.'

Muhammad, Ali and Abdullah, filled with excitement and wonder, waited to hear the rest of the story. Their father continued. "The king waited for a short while, but the young man did not come out of the cave. So he waited a little longer, and still neither he nor the other young believers emerged. "Finally," said their father slowly and dramatically, "the king and his soldiers entered the cave and found all of the young believers lying there ... dead."

The boys were speechless. Their father continued in the same carefully measured tones.

"The good king and his men were astonished, but they realised something very important."

'This is a sign of Allah's great power,' said the king. 'I must return to the city and seek the advice of my ministers, as to the meaning of this miracle.'

"The king left some men to stand guard at the cave. Then he and his remaining soldiers returned to the city in haste, each of them filled with awe at what they had witnessed. The king wasted no time in calling his ministers to discuss the situation and what to do about it."

"One of his ministers said: 'The cave is similar to the grave, and this story is an excellent reminder to us all that we shall die, enter the grave, and then wake up on the Day of Judgement.'

'I wonder why Allah didn't let them die in their own time as people usually do,' the king mused.

'Instead, they were made to sleep all the while. Perhaps that was to strengthen our faith in the will and power of Allah?'

"I believe your majesty is correct," said another minister.

"Why doesn't your majesty build a memorial over the cave and leave them buried inside it?"

"I will build a house of worship near the site of the cave, for the worship of Allah alone,' decided the king. 'When people go there to pray it will serve as a reminder for them of Allah's power.'

"And that is the story of the People of the Cave," said their father to Abdullah, Ali and Muhammad, who were fascinated by what they had heard. He gazed at them one by one, noting their looks of astonishment, and asked, "What do you think Allah wants to teach us through this story in the Qur'an? "

The boys thought carefully before replying.

"It teaches us that believers should protect their faith by any means they can," replied Ali.

His father nodded in agreement.

Muhammad said, "That Allah always is on the side of believers and will not abandon them."

"And," Abdullah added, "No matter how strong injustice may seem, it will always be defeated in the end. Faith overcomes all obstacles."

"Faith overcomes all obstacles!" repeated Ali and Muhammad in unison.

"Yes, my sons," agreed their father. "You are right," their mother joined in.

"You know, Mama," admitted Muhammad, "In the beginning I was afraid that the believers might change their faith, because the king ordered them to do so."

"There is a saying that even the strong wind of injustice can't blow out the burning flame of faith in the believer's heart," replied their mother. "The evil king was wrong when he thought he could force faith out of the young men's hearts with the edge of his sword. You can never really change a person's beliefs by force. That's why the Qur'an says 'there is no compulsion in religion.' "

"Another important lesson Allah wants to show us with this story," added their father, "is that although people are always arguing about who is right, most of what they say is conjecture, or 'educated guesswork'. Many legends had sprung up about the People of the Cave by the time of the Prophet ﷺ. The Christians claimed them as their own, calling them the 'Seven Sleepers of Ephesus', whereas the Jews believed that they were from their people, possibly belonging to the religious community known as Essenes. To argue about what city they came from, which king it was that persecuted them, how many of them there were, or exactly how long they slept, is to miss the point of the story."

"I would like to read this story in the Qur'an myself, tomorrow," said Abdullah. "I will read it before we go to the mosque for Friday prayers, *insha' Allah*."

"Me too," said his younger brothers, in unison.

"*Masha' Allah*," said their father. "Nothing is by accident in this world. Did you boys know that it is especially recommended to read *Surah al-Kahf* on a Friday? The Prophet ﷺ said that whoever reads it on one Friday will have the light of heaven shine on him until the next Friday. It is a fascinating *surah*, and contains a number of other stories as well."

"Excellent!" exclaimed Abdullah.

Their father then said, "I pray that Allah will continue to

bless each of you and increase your understanding of the *din* (religion). Tomorrow we can read *Surah al-Kahf* together, *insha' Allah*. Now, let's get ready for *'Isha'* prayers."

THE QUR'ANIC STORY OF
THE PEOPLE OF THE CAVE

In the name of Allah, the Most Compassionate, the Most Merciful

Surah al-Kahf (Chapter 18)

Verse

9 Do you think that the People of the Cave and the Inscription were one of Our wondrous signs?

10 When those youths sought refuge in the Cave and said: 'Our Lord! Grant us mercy from Yourself and provide for us rectitude in our affairs',

11 We lulled them to sleep in that cave for a number of years

12 And then awakened them so that We might see which of the two parties could best tell the length of their stay.

13 We narrate to you their true story. They were a party of young men who had faith in their Lord, and We increased them in guidance.

14 And strengthened their hearts when they stood up and proclaimed: 'Our Lord is the Lord of the heavens and the earth. We shall call upon no other god beside Him; (for if we did so), we shall be uttering a blasphemy.'

41

15 (Then they conferred among themselves and said): 'These men, our own people, have taken others as gods beside Him: why do they not bring any clear evidence that they indeed are gods? Who can be more unjust than he who foists a lie on Allah?

16 And now that you have dissociated yourselves from them and from whatever they worship beside Allah, go and seek refuge in the Cave. Your Lord will extend His mercy to you and will provide for you the means for the disposal of your affairs.'

17 Had you looked at them in the Cave it would have appeared to you that when the sun rose, it moved away from their cave to the right; and when it set, it turned away from them to the left, while they remained in a spacious hollow in the Cave. This is one of the Signs of Allah. Whomsoever Allah guides, he alone is led aright; and whomsoever Allah lets go astray, you will find for him no guardian to direct him.

18 On seeing them you would fancy them to be awake though they were asleep; and We caused them to turn their sides to their right and to their left, and their dog sat stretching out its two forelegs on the threshold of the Cave. Had you looked upon them you would have certainly fled away from them, their sight filling you with terror.

19 *Likewise, We roused them in a miraculous way that they might question one another. One of them asked: 'How long did you remain (in this state)?'*
The others said: 'We remained so for a day, or part of a day.'
Then they said: 'Your Lord knows better how long we remained in this state. Now send one of us to the city with this coin of ours and let him see who has the best food, and let him buy some provisions from there. Let him be cautious and not inform anyone of our whereabouts.

20 *For if they should come upon us, they will stone us to death or force us to revert to their faith whereafter we shall never prosper.'*

21 *Thus did We make their case known to the people of the city so that they might know that Allah's promise is true, and that there is absolutely no doubt that the Hour will come to pass. But instead of giving thought to this, they disputed with one another concerning the People of the Cave, some saying: 'Build a wall over them. Their Lord alone knows best about them.' But those who prevailed over their affairs said: 'We shall build a place of worship over them.'*

22 *Some will say concerning them: 'They were three and their dog, the fourth'; and some will say: 'They were five and their dog, the sixth' – all this being merely guesswork; and still others will say: 'They were seven, and their dog, the*

43

eighth.' Say: 'My Lord knows their correct number. So, do not dispute concerning their number, except cursorily, and do not question anyone about them.

23 And never say about anything: "I shall certainly do this tomorrow."

24 Unless Allah should will it. And should you forget, (and make such a statement), remember your Lord and say: "I expect my Lord to guide me to what is nearer to rectitude than this."'

25 They remained in the Cave for three hundred years; and some others add nine more years.

26 Say: 'Allah knows best how long they remained in it; for only He knows all that is hidden in the heavens and the earth. How well He sees; how well He hears! The creatures have no other guardian than Him; He allows none to share His authority.*

* Sayyid Abul A`la Mawdudi, *Towards Understanding the Quran*. Translated and edited by Zafar Ishaq Ansari, The Islamic Foundation, Leicester, 1995. Vol. V, pp. 89-101.